For Henry (10,500 miles south),
Callum (150 miles west)
and Simon (just down the road!)

First published in
Great Britain in 2010
by Egmont UK Limited
239 Kensington High Street
London W8 6SA

ISBN – 978 1 4052 4826 6 (Hardback)
ISBN – 978 1 4052 4825 9 (Paperback)
All rights reserved
10 9 8 7 6 5 4 3 2 1
Printed in Singapore

HOLD ON TIGHT, STRIPY HORSE!

Jim Helmore and Karen Wall

EGMONT

SPLISH! SPLASH! SPLOSH!

Wet and windy magic was at work in the bric-a-brac shop.

PLOP!

A big drop of icy water landed
on the stripy horse's nose
and woke him up.

"It's raining **indoors!**" he shivered.

"Wiggle in your wellies!"
splashed Roly and Pitch.

"Hang on to your hats!"
chirped Muriel.

"And bring out
your brollies!"
barked Hermann.

"Did someone call?"
A flamingo-shaped umbrella
stepped out of the basket by the door.
"My name's Ella," she smiled.
"You can shelter under me if you like."

They all crowded underneath Ella's enormous wings. The rain was getting heavier.

"We've got to put a stop to this!"

said the soggy stripy horse.

Suddenly a great
gust of wind
blew across
the shop
and lifted Ella
into the air.

The stripy horse
grabbed Ella . . .

WHOOSH!

... and
Hermann grabbed
the stripy horse,
but the wind was
too strong for them.

They were whisked
off the ground!

Up and up they rushed . . .

past the puzzle chest . . .

and the cuckoo clock . . .

and over the counter at the front of the shop.

The water was rising fast.
Soon Roly and Pitch
were paddling in a snaking,
bubbling stream.

"Hold on tight,
stripy horse!"

they cried.

SWiSH!

Ella was blown towards a picture
on the wall ahead.

The crashing,
flashing painting
was spraying
rain and snow
all over the shop!

"I've never seen a picture like **that** before!" said the stripy horse.

"It's called 'Tropical Paradise'," frowned Muriel.

"Doesn't look much like paradise to me," woofed Hermann.

THUD!

The friends landed
on a bookshelf.

"What a ride!"
said the stripy horse.
"But at least we've
found out where the rain
is coming from!"

"THE NORTH WIND WILL BLOW AND WE SHALL HAVE SNOW!" warned a squawking voice.

They all peered over the side of the shelf and saw a fat, metal bird on an odd-looking perch.

N
E

"That's the weathervane parrot,"
said Muriel. "He points in
the direction of the wind
but he's stuck facing north and
a north wind brings snow and rain."

"So that's why it's raining in the picture!" cried the stripy horse.

"Oh my goodness!" called Ella. **"Look down there!"**

Far below, Roly and Pitch were being swept towards a waterfall that **dashed** and **splashed** down the steps to the shop's basement!

"Man overboard!" cried Roly.

"Quick, everyone!"
said the stripy horse.
"We'll have to unstick the parrot
and point him back the other way.
If we all join together, I think
we can just reach across!"

"LOOK BEFORE YOU LEAP!"
cried the parrot.

Hermann swung

and the stripy horse **stretched**

but Ella couldn't hook the parrot's beak.
"SOS!" shouted Pitch from the river.

"IF AT FIRST YOU DON'T SUCCEED

"TRY, TRY AGAIN!" screeched the parrot.

"Don't worry," said the stripy horse. "I'm very good with feathery objects!"

SWOOSH!

They swung again.

The stripy horse s t r e t c h e d
until he thought he would split a seam . . .

. . . and with a
clink of metal,
Ella hooked
the parrot!

"Hurray!"
cried the penguins
from the water below.

"Now PULL, everyone!"
twittered Muriel.

"ONE GOOD TURN
DESERVES
ANOTHER!"
called the parrot,
and he creaked
and groaned around
to face the other way.

But as the parrot turned,
Ella lost her grip and the friends swung backwards!

HELLLLPPPPP!

"WHAT
GOES UP
MUST COME
DOWN!"
squawked
the parrot.

BANG!

They crashed into
the shelf behind
them . . .

. . . and began to fall,

down,

down,

down!

Ella opened her wings just in time.

And they floated through the air . . .

. . . landing with a gentle splosh in the river below.

With some speedy
doggy paddling . . .

"Ahoy there!"
cried the penguins.

. . . the stripy horse scooped up Roly and Pitch

just before they were swept over the basement steps.

"What kept you?"

asked the penguins.

The rain had stopped, the wind had dropped
and the shop was drying out.

Up in the painting, sunlight sparkled on the gentle waves
and flying fish leapt into the sky.

"It's a **proper**
tropical paradise again,"
said the stripy horse.

Roly and Pitch pulled out some deck chairs
and they all settled down
in the picture's golden glow.

"ALL'S WELL THAT ENDS WELL!"

squawked the weathervane parrot.